A 20th Century Fox Presentation

ANASTASIA

A Don Bluth / Gary Goldman Fi

D1119523

Together in Paris

adapted by
Melissa Peterson

illustrated by
Alan Nowell & Associates

🐾 A GOLDEN BOOK • NEW YORK

Golden Books Publishing Company, Inc. New York, New York 10106

Library of Congress Catalog Card Number: 97-74208   ISBN: 0-307-20013-2
A MCMXCVII

Anya was a girl with a mystery to solve.
She had lived in an orphanage
since she was eight years old.
She did not know who her parents were.
Her only clue to the past was a necklace
with a gold key on it.
On the key were the words:
"Together in Paris."

Now Anya was eighteen.
It was time for her to leave the orphanage.
"Maybe I should go to Paris,"
she said to the headmistress.
"Maybe there I can find out
who my family is."

"Family?" said the headmistress.
"You have no family! You are an orphan.
The only place you will be going is
the fish factory!
I got you a job there.
Forget about Paris!"

Anya was sad.
Maybe the headmistress was right.
She said good-bye and set off
down the road to the fish factory.
But she could not stop thinking
about the words on the necklace.
"Together in Paris"—what did it mean?

She came to a crossroads.
The fish factory was one way.
The other road led
to the city of St. Petersburg.
In St. Petersburg
she could take a train to Paris.
Anya stared at the signs.
She did not know which way to go.

"Woof!" A little dog ran up to Anya. "Woof!"
The dog grabbed her scarf in his teeth.
He ran a little way down the path
to St. Petersburg.
"Hey!" Anya cried. "Give me that!"
But the dog ran further down the path.
He looked back at Anya, wagging his tail.

"It's a sign," Anya said to herself.
"This dog is trying to tell me to go
to St. Petersburg!"
She made up her mind.
"All right," she told the dog. "I'll do it!
I'll take a train to Paris.
I'm going to find my family!"

But in St. Petersburg, Anya found
that train tickets were hard to find.
She met two men named
Dimitri and Vladimir.
They had an extra ticket to Paris.
But it was for the long-lost princess
named Anastasia.

Dimitri told Anya about how the princess
had disappeared during an attack
on the palace many years ago.
All these years, the princess's grandmother,
the empress Marie, had lived in Paris.
Marie had been hoping for the return of
her Anastasia.
Dimitri had looked all over St. Petersburg,
hoping to find the princess Anastasia.

Dimitri stared at Anya.
"You know," he said,
"you look a lot like Anastasia!
The same eyes, the same hands..."
Vladimir added,
"And you're just the right age!"
"You must be crazy!" Anya laughed.
"Me, a princess? I'm just an orphan girl."

"But you don't remember anything
about your past,"
Dimitri pointed out.
"You should at least talk
to Empress Marie.
Maybe she can help you remember!"
Anya thought hard.
Maybe it wasn't such a crazy idea after all.
"All right, I'll do it!" she agreed.

And so they set out.
They took a train and a boat.
Finally they reached Paris—
the city Anya had dreamed of all her life.
"Oh!" she whispered to her little dog,
"maybe here I will learn the truth about
my family."

Vladimir took Anya to see
a woman named Sophie.
Sophie was the cousin
of Empress Marie.
The only way to meet the empress was
to make Sophie believe that Anya was
the lost princess, Anastasia.

"She certainly does look like the princess,"
said Sophie.
"But then, so do all the others."
"What others?" Anya asked.
Sophie rolled her eyes. "Oh, my dear,
there have been dozens of girls
who think they are the princess.
All of them have turned out to be fakes."

"Oh, my," said Anya.
"Indeed," said Sophie.
"I hope you won't mind
answering a few questions for me.
Let's see . . . Where were you born?"

Dimitri had told Anya just what to say.
"In Peterhoff Palace," said Anya.
"Right," Sophie said.
"What color was Count Sergei's cat?"
"Yellow," said Anya.
The questions went on and on.
Thanks to Dimitri,
Anya knew all the answers.

"One last question," Sophie said.
"How did you escape
during the attack on the palace?"
Dimitri and Vladimir turned pale.
They had not told Anya the answer.
But Anya said softly, "There was a boy
who worked at the palace.
He opened a secret door in the wall."

Dimitri gasped.
He had been that servant boy!
But he had never told anyone
about the secret door.
Now he knew Anya really was
the lost princess.
Sophie believed it, too.
"Marie will be at the ballet
tonight,"
she said. "Meet us there!"

At the ballet, Anya waited outside
while Dimitri talked to Marie.
Anya was so excited!
Soon she would meet
the woman who might be her
grandmother.
But Dimitri came outside
with some bad news.
Marie would not see Anya.
"I have seen enough pretenders
to last a lifetime," Marie had said.
"Hasn't my heart been broken enough?"

Anya's own heart sank.
If Marie would not see her,
how would she ever learn the truth?
"I guess you are all the family I've got,"
she said to her little dog, Pooka.
"Come on," she said.
"Let's go back to Sophie's house
and pack our things."

Dimitri felt terrible.

He knew Anya's heart was breaking.

"She really is the princess,"
he said to himself.

"She doesn't know it, but I'm the boy
who helped her escape all those years ago."

He remembered how Anastasia had fled into
the night, dropping something as she ran.

Suddenly, Dimitri had an idea.
That night, he pretended to be
the driver of Marie's car.
"Please listen to me,"
he begged the empress.
"I have found the real Anastasia.
Please talk to her."
"No!" said Marie.

Dimitri handed Marie a small box.
"Have you seen this before?" he asked.
It was a music box.
It was what Anastasia had dropped
as she ran through the secret door.
For all these years, Dimitri had kept it safe.

Marie stared at the box.
Her eyes filled with tears.
She had given that music box
to Anastasia many years ago.
"Where did you get this?"
she asked Dimitri.
"Please just talk to Anya," Dimitri pleaded.

Back at Sophie's house, Anya was packing.
Someone knocked on the door.
Anya could not believe her eyes—
it was Empress Marie!
Marie looked Anya up and down.
"Who are you?" the old woman asked.

Anya sighed.
"I was hoping you could tell me," she said.
"But I guess I was wrong."
She turned away sadly.
Suddenly she sniffed.
There was a faint, sweet smell in the air.
"Peppermint?" Anya asked.

"An oil for my hands," Marie explained.
Anya gasped.
She remembered!
"When I was little, I spilled a bottle!"
she cried.
"The rug was soaked.
After that it always smelled like—you!"

Anya stared at Marie in wonder.
Her hand went to the gold key at her neck.
Marie's eyes were wide.
"May I see that key?" she asked.
Her voice was trembling.

Marie took out the music box
Dimitri had given her.
Anya's key fit just right.
Marie wound the box,
and a soft song began to play.
"This was our secret," Marie said.
"My Anastasia's and mine...."

Memories came rushing back to Anya.
"The song!" she exclaimed.
"You used to sing it to me!"
"Anastasia! My Anastasia!" Marie cried.
"It's really you!"
She threw her arms around Anya
in a big hug.
Anya felt as though she would
float off the ground.
She had found her grandmother.
They were together in Paris—at last.